Mad about

Ballet

written by Lisa Regan
illustrated by Sue Hendra and Paul Linnet

consultant: Dawn King LCDD, RAD, RTS
Director of Gedling Ballet School

A catalogue record for this book is available from the British Library

Published by Ladybird Books Ltd
80 Strand London WC2R 0RL
A Penguin Company

2 4 6 8 10 9 7 5 3 1
© LADYBIRD BOOKS LTD MMVIII
LADYBIRD and the device of a Ladybird are trademarks of Ladybird Books Ltd

Produced by Calcium for Ladybird Books Ltd

ISBN: 9781 84646 925 1

Printed in China

Contents

Some words appear in **bold** in this book.
Turn to the glossary to learn about them.

Welcome to the ballet

Ballet is a beautiful form of dancing. It tells stories to music. Ballet began about 500 years ago, in Italy.

Ballet became very popular in France 400 years ago. That is why many of the words used to describe ballet are French.

Ballet dancers have very fit bodies. They can balance and bend far more than any ordinary person.

A **choreographer** (*kor-ee-og-raf-er*) is the person in charge of planning the dance moves in a ballet.

The word 'ballet' is also used to describe a performance. People say they are 'going to the ballet'.

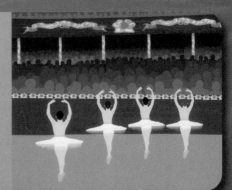

7

Getting Started

Children can begin to learn ballet when they are very young. As dancers grow older, they learn harder moves. To become a **professional**, dancers train very hard, usually from the age of ten.

A ballet class always begins with exercises to warm up the dancers' muscles. Dancers also perform gentle stretches.

A ballet dancer's **posture** is very important. A dancer's body should stretch upwards at all times.

bad posture

good posture

Very little is needed to start ballet. A **leotard** and soft shoes are the most important things. Socks, tights and a cardigan help to keep dancers warm.

Basic positions

One of the first things a ballet dancer learns is the basic **positions**. These are five foot and arm **poses**.

First position

Arms are held in a gentle, curved position

Legs are turned outwards from the hips

When children first learn ballet they do not stand with their legs and feet fully turned out. This takes some time to learn.

Toes and feet are turned outwards

Heels are kept together

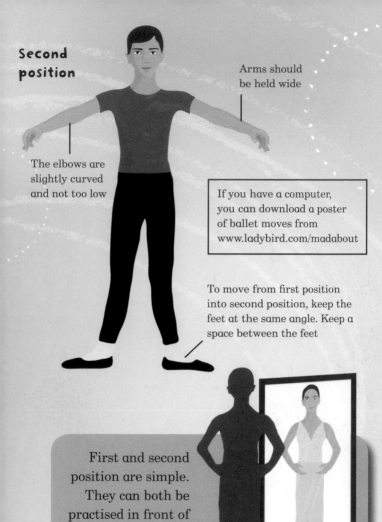

Second position

Arms should be held wide

The elbows are slightly curved and not too low

If you have a computer, you can download a poster of ballet moves from www.ladybird.com/madabout

To move from first position into second position, keep the feet at the same angle. Keep a space between the feet

First and second position are simple. They can both be practised in front of a mirror at home.

Harder positions

The basic positions get harder and harder. Some teachers start with the arms, then move on to the foot positions later.

Third position

One arm is held in first position and one in second

Fourth position

The front arm is held above the head in a graceful curve. The other arm is still held to the side

One foot is placed in front of the other. The front heel should be halfway along the back foot

One foot is positioned exactly in front of the other, with a space between the feet

Fifth position

Both arms are held above the head ———

Arms should frame the face

The feet move together from fourth position to fifth position

Feet should be crossed, with legs turned outwards

13

Practice makes perfect

A dance studio has a rail on the wall called a ***barre*** (*bar*). Dancers hold onto the *barre* when stretching, balancing and practising ballet moves.

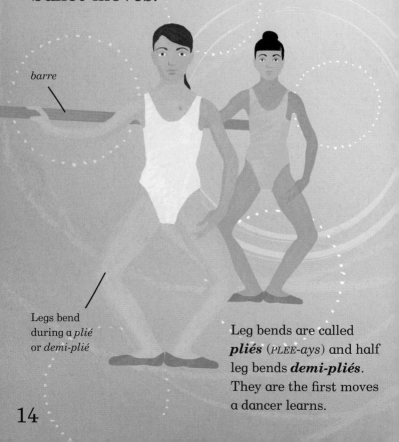

barre

Legs bend during a *plié* or *demi-plié*

Leg bends are called ***pliés*** (PLEE-*ays*) and half leg bends ***demi-pliés***. They are the first moves a dancer learns.

Ballet movements should be done with pointed feet. That makes a dancer's legs look longer and more graceful.

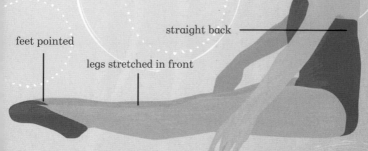

straight back

feet pointed

legs stretched in front

The **pirouette** (*pi-roo-ET*) is a favourite move. Dancers perform it by spinning on one leg.

With skill and practice, almost every ballet move can be performed **en tournant** (*on-TOOR-non*), or turning. That allows the dancer to move around the floor.

Dancing together

When two people dance together it is called *pas de deux* (*pa-de-DUH*). Together, the dancers can perform incredible steps and lifts.

An ***arabesque*** (*a-reb-ESK*) is a wonderful ballet balance. The male dancer sometimes supports the female in an *arabesque* ***en pointe*** (*on-point*), which means on tiptoes.

en pointe

The male dancer must be very strong, so he can hold his partner in the air.

A whole group of dancers often perform the same steps at the same time. The group is called the ***corps de ballet*** (*cor-de-*BAL*-ay*). Their movements make beautiful patterns.

17

Ballet shoes

Dancers wear ballet shoes made of leather, satin or canvas when they first begin their training. The shoes are held on the feet with elastic or ribbons.

A dancer must learn to tie his or her ballet shoes properly. This can take some practice. Both ribbons are crossed in front of and behind the leg, near the ankle. They should be tied neatly on the inside of the leg.

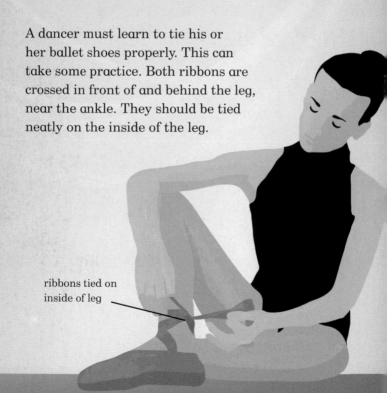

ribbons tied on inside of leg

Special *pointe* shoes are needed to dance *en pointe*. They have hard toes and strong **soles**. *Pointe* shoes can be painful to wear if they do not fit correctly. Some dancers use padding to protect their toes inside the shoe.

ribbons are hand-sewn onto shoes and then cut to the right length

teacher

pupil

Teachers can tell when their pupils' feet and bodies are strong enough to work *en pointe*.

19

Ballet school

Ballet school is for dancers
who want to move on from
ballet classes and learn more.
An audition, or test, must be
passed before a dancer is offered
a place at ballet school.

Dancers must keep their hair tidy.
Long hair is tied back so it does not
fall across the dancer's face or eyes.

Ballet teachers help their pupils to warm up. They might play games to warm up, such as pretending to be animals or fairy tale **characters**.

Ballet pupils learn how to fit their movements to the music. Marching and clapping in time is good practice.

Girl dancers **curtsey** to their teacher at the end of a class.

21

Ballet costumes

Ballet costumes are designed to tell the audience about the characters in a ballet. They also show off the movements of the dance.

This pretty net dress is called a **tutu** (*too-too*).

All ballet costumes are designed to help dancers move as easily as possible.

The costumes of the main characters in a ballet are often a different colour to the costumes of the other dancers. That makes the main characters stand out.

Some ballets use amazing costumes. In the ballet *The Tales of Beatrix Potter*, all the dancers are dressed in animal costumes.

Going to the ballet

A trip to the theatre to see a ballet performance is a magical experience.

Many **classical ballets** tell traditional stories, such as fairy tales. Some ballets tell love stories.

The Nutcracker is a fairy tale

Modern ballets do not always have a story. Instead, the dancers use their movements to show feelings and **emotions**.

Ballet dancers use their body shapes and their faces to show their characters' feelings or what is happening in the story.

Famous ballets

Swan Lake
This ballet tells the story of
Princess Odette, who is turned
into a swan by a sorcerer. ——

The Nutcracker
A beautiful ballet about a
magical Christmas present.

The Dream
A ballet based on Shakespeare's
A Midsummer Night's Dream.

Sleeping Beauty
This famous ballet tells
the story of a princess woken
from a spell by the kiss
of a prince.

Romeo and Juliet

A romantic ballet based on Shakespeare's play.

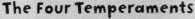

Les Noces (The Wedding)

This ballet tells the story of a wedding in a poor Russian family nearly one hundred years ago.

The Four Temperaments

This is a modern ballet. It looks at different feelings, such as sadness and happiness.

The Prince of the Pagodas

This modern ballet tells the story of an ancient emperor and his daughters.

The Tales of Beatrix Potter

This ballet is based on the animal stories in Beatrix Potter's books.

Coppelia

In this ballet, a toymaker is tricked into thinking that one of his dolls has come to life.

27

Simply the best

⭐ Anna Pavlova

1881–1931
This Russian ballerina was famous for her graceful performances. She helped to design the *pointe* shoe used by most modern ballerinas.

⭐ Fonteyn and Nureyev

Dame Margot Fonteyn (1919–1991) and Rudolf Nureyev (1938–1993) danced beautifully alone, but together they were the world's most famous partnership.

Alicia Markova

1910–2004
This English *prima ballerina* (leading lady) formed her own ballet company in 1950. It later became the English National Ballet.

Vaslav Nijinsky

1890–1950
This male ballet dancer will always be remembered for his powerful body and great dance routines.

Darcey Bussell

1969–present
Darcey was 13 years old when she began serious training. She has shown that a ballet dancer can begin dancing when they are older and still become a great dancer.

Glossary

arabesque – a balance on one leg, with the other leg stretched out straight behind.

barre – a rail or double rail attached to the wall of a ballet studio.

character – a made up person in a play or story.

choreographer – the person who puts dance moves together to form a dance.

classical ballet – an older ballet technique from hundreds of years ago.

corps de ballet – dancers that perform together as a group.

curtsey – when a girl or woman bends her knees and bows her head.

demi-plié – a half-bend at the knees.

emotions – feelings.

en pointe – standing raised on the tips of the toes wearing special shoes.

en tournant – a move which turns the dancer around.

leotard – a special piece of stretchy clothing, a little like a swimsuit.

modern ballet – a type of ballet developed over the last hundred or so years.

pirouette – a complete turn of the body on one foot.

plié – a bend at the knees.

pose – a position a dancer stands in.

positions – five basic ways of placing the arms and feet in ballet.

posture – the way a dancer holds his or her body.

professional – when someone is fully trained to do something for a living.

soles – the undersides of the feet or bottom of shoes.

tutu – a dress with a frilly net skirt worn in ballet.